# CLINICAL RESEARCH
## TRIALS AND TRIUMPHS

*A heart warming novel following
a nurse's journey into clinical research*

Elizabeth Weeks-Rowe

# About The Author

Elizabeth Blair Weeks-Rowe, LVN, CCRA, has spent 14 years in a variety of clinical research roles, such as Clinical Research Associate (CRA), CRA trainer, CRA manager and business development director. She has written and edited newsletters for several Clinical Research Organizations (CRO), created training curriculum for CRA/clinical research educational and training programs and has contributed website content for several research programs. She has been published in a number of clinical research magazines, and writes a monthly column for a large clinical research on line/print publication.

# Clinical Research Trials and Triumphs
A heart warming novel following a nurse's
journey into clinical research

ISBN: 978-0-692-31798-3

Published by Elizabeth Weeks-Rowe
California, USA

Print layout and interior design by Booknook.biz

# DISCLAIMER

This is a work of fiction. While, as in all fiction, the literary perceptions and insights are based on experience, all names, characters, places, and incidents are either products of the author's imagination or are used fictitiously. No reference to any real persons is intended or should be inferred.

Although this is purely a work of fiction it does contain terminology, references, places and situations that are related to the medical, pharmaceutical and health care industries. Please note that this book and any information within it, is designed to entertain the reader on the subjects discussed. This book is not meant to be used, nor should it be used, to diagnose or treat any medical condition. For diagnosis or treatment of any medical problem, consult your own physician. The publisher and author are not responsible for needs that may require medical supervision and are not liable for any damages or negative health related consequences to any person reading this book. Any references are provided for entertainment purposes only and do not constitute an endorsement.

# CHAPTER

## 1

# SO DO YOU KNOW ANYTHING ABOUT CLINICAL RESEARCH?

"So, do you know anything about clinical research?" This was the pivotal question that, unbeknownst to me at the time, would define the start of my career in clinical research. I walked into the recruiting office of a large medical clinic in my home town, seeking employment as a nurse. Did I mention that I was fresh out of nursing school, and ridiculously naïve and idealistic? After the requisite pleasantries with the recruiter, I began my unfortunate interviewing spiel. I explained that I became a nurse to help people, (how original), and that I believed working at the clinic would enable me to make a positive impact on patients' lives. The recruiter shot me a speculative glance, and raised her eyebrows as if to say, (insert sarcastic tone) "Really? I have never heard that before…"

Her next sentence would literally change my life. "So, do you know anything about clinical research?" she asked. Externally, I was speechless, but with a mad internal dialogue. Had the recruiter paid attention to anything I had just said? How did clinical research have anything to do with nursing? Did I resemble a mad scientist, with the proverbial white coat and wild hair? What in the world was clinical research, anyway? I informed the recruiter that I did not have any research experience, but that I was, OF COURSE, interested in learning new things. Looking back, I think I would have said anything to get a job, and pay off my student loans.

"Great, come with me," she declared, as if I had a choice. She then took my hand and dragged me down two flights of stairs to the office of a female internal medicine physician, Dr. Smith. We stood in the doorway of Dr. Smith's office for what seemed an eternity. Dr. Smith finally looked up from her massive mahogany desk and motioned for us to enter. The recruiter informed Dr. Smith that she had a possible candidate for the research coordinator position and asked if she were available for a quick chat. Dr. Smith looked directly into my eyes, for what seemed like an eternity. Though I felt very uncomfortable, I was determined to keep eye contact (I cursed my traitorous eyelid as it began to twitch nervously). Her face was inscrutable as she continued to stare at me. She was an attractive, thin female of indeterminate middle age. She was dressed in an expensive business suit, underneath a white doctor's coat. She had an air of accomplishment and authority that intimidated me. I swallowed and wondered what I had gotten myself into? After what seemed like forever, Dr. Smith finally broke eye contact and turned back to her computer screen to finish typing something undoubtedly important. The recruiter and I stood there awkwardly. Dr. Smith then rose, grabbed several charts from her desk and turned to exit the office. My first thought was that she had found me a deficient candidate, based on that five minute once-over, and that this was her way of dismissing me from her presence. Instead, she surprised me by asking, nay commanding us, to follow her. "Walk with me" were her exact words. We naturally obeyed.

I would later discover that Dr. Smith had a way of compelling people to follow her commands. This always intrigued me about her. She walked swiftly down the hallway, and we literally had to sprint to catch up to her. She had a purposeful stride, like I imagined a busy doctor would, and it was difficult to maintain her pace, let alone conversation. The conversation, or interview, went as follows: Dr. Smith (calm demeanor, even tone of voice, yet incredibly intimidating) said to me, "Do you have any clinical research experience?" The recruiter responded (though the question was directed at me, apparently the recruiter was speaking on my behalf). "Lisa does not have any research experience, but she does have nursing experience." Really, I did? I was thinking SO loudly to myself...How did the recruiter know what, if any, nursing experience I had? She hadn't even bothered to look at my Curriculum Vitae (CV). Dr. Smith nodded briskly, and kept nodding throughout the entire conversation; in which I had very little participation, though I was the primary subject. After walking for about five minutes, Dr. Smith stopped short of a wing of administrative offices. She looked sternly into my eyes, "Lisa, I need a study coordinator who is dependable and willing to work hard. I hope you can be that person." And what was my brilliant response? To smile and nod my head vigorously. It seems I had lost my ability to speak during the walk from Dr. Smith's office to her pod of examination rooms. She gave me one last lingering look, and disappeared into an exam room.

I was a little confused. Dr. Smith's final words to me were promising, but without substance, as they did not include an offer of employment. I glanced anxiously at the recruiter, for I had no idea what had just happened. Was this a casual "get to know you" conversation, or a formal interview? During the discourse, I contributed nothing tangible, but merely nodded my head like a silly puppet.

As we walked back up the stairs to the recruiter's office, I noticed she had resumed her perfect human resources poker face, aka "the smile that did not reach the eyes." I had a million questions, but knew it was not appropriate to ask any of them. I wanted to scream, jump in the air, and flail madly-- anything to get a confirmation from the recruiter over what had taken place with Dr. Smith. But the recruiter's expression was set in stone. When we reached her office, I shook her hand, and thanked her for her time. She smiled that same artificial smile, and gave me the token "we will be in touch" farewell that told me basically, nothing.

In touch for what? I wanted to scream. WHAT HAD JUST HAPPENED???

I had just completed what I thought was an interview, about a position that I had never heard of, nor knew anything about. Great…I had been searching for a job to sink my teeth and ambition into, and if it turned out to be terrible, after a year or two I could move into a more interesting department. I just needed to get an actual job, to pay my rent, bills, and to get my nagging mother off of my back.

Millions of questions/random thoughts were swimming in my head as I drove home from the impromptu interview. I did not think that walking swiftly down a hallway, watching a busy physician and a determined recruiter talk about you, constituted an interview, according to state law. I did not know if I had been offered the job. I had not filled out any employment paperwork, let alone an application. If I worked for Dr. Smith I would definitely have to learn to walk faster. What exactly would I be doing if I they offered me the job? Studying bacteria under a microscope? Would I have to buy a microscope? I did not have the funds for that, which meant I would have to ask my mother for the money, something I always dreaded doing.

When I arrived home, I collapsed on my bed, exhausted by the events of the day. I was asleep within minutes. I was awakened several hours later by a phone call from that poker faced recruiter, offering me the position. I said yes before she could change her mind, before even considering what I had gotten myself into.

# CHAPTER

## 2

## WELCOME TO THE JUNGLE.

I wish I could tell you that my first day as a study coordinator was smooth and uneventful. That could not have been farther from the truth. I arrived at the clinic at 7:30 am, after a sleepless night spent worrying over a job I had not yet even started (what if I don't understand things... what if I make a mistake, can a person get fired on the first day?). I had an 8:30 a.m. human resources appointment, so I found a coffee cart at the clinic entrance, and spent the next 45 minutes drinking a latte. The caffeine just made me more jittery. At 8:15 am, I went to the ladies restroom for a final appearance check before my appointment. My mother always stressed the importance of a first impression; I had punctuality covered, but needed to ensure that my appearance was likewise appropriate for the first day of my new career. The mirror was not feeling particularly charitable. Dark circles and drawn skin don't go well with conservative business attire. I looked edgy and tired, but there was nothing I could do about that now. I applied fresh lip gloss, straightened my shoulders, and made my way to the human resources office.

When I opened the door to the office, a buzzer sounded, and yet no one appeared at the front desk. I sat on a chair in the lobby and waited for someone to appear, to check me in. Fifteen minutes later, a middle aged woman with glasses walked quickly towards me from the back hallway. She looked even more stressed out than I felt. "Are you Lisa?" she asked me. I nodded and started to introduce myself. Before I could form the first word, she interrupted me. "I'm Jane, the research supervisor. Come with me please." No hand extended, no cheerful greeting. Just another bossy female who walked fast. I was starting to see a pattern here. I dutifully followed Jane down a long hallway and made a mental note to invest in a sturdy pair of cross trainers. The hallway ended at a long row of administrative offices. We entered the last office on the right, presumably belonging to Jane. She motioned for me to take a seat across from her desk. After a long, dramatic sigh, Jane explained "our little problem," or, AKA, "Dr. Smith's alternative training plan."

Jane was an awful actress. She was clearly annoyed, attempting to mask it with feigned concern for my situation. "There is a training process all new research employees must complete, and Dr. Smith is aware of this. SOPs, new hire paperwork and computer training are completed by all new hires their first week of employment." She looked as if she expected me to understand all of this. I opted with the silent nodding thing that I did during my initial interview with Dr. Smith and the recruiter. That seemed to work well for me when I had no idea what was going on. Jane sighed again and continued her explanation. "Dr. Smith has scheduled a monitoring visit for today. This is most inappropriate for a first day." Her mouth formed into a disapproving frown with this declaration. She then turned to me. For, for, FOR WHAT? I longed to shout. Commiseration? Empathy? One has to understand said topic to form an opinion, much less a sympathetic one. I had no idea what she was talking about. What in the heck was a monitoring visit?

Jane continued to stare at me, clearly waiting for some response. I started to feel uncomfortable, and began to study my shoelaces, the polyester couch cushions, the dated, floral wallpaper, anything to avoid eye contact. I don't know what she expected from me. I was here to complete new hire forms, and learn a new position. I had no idea why she was throwing around research terms and policy, as if I could relate. I had been candid with the recruiter about my absolute lack of research experience. The recruiter had been candid with Dr. Smith about my lack of research experience. It had seemed like a non-issue, especially considering that I had been offered a position. And then clarity hit me like a resounding slap in the face. No-one had been candid with Jane about my lack of research experience. Now, this was my problem.

While I racked my brain for any solution, Jane rose from her desk. "Well, I guess I will need to have one of the other study coordinators sit with the monitor until you are ready." That poor study coordinator was going to be "sitting with the monitor" for a very long time, unless I told Jane the truth about my lack of experience. "Jane" I began awkwardly. "Um… I don't know if anyone told you, but I don't have any research experience." Her disapproving frown quickly turned to disapproving surprise. It quickly became very important for me to explain the situation to Jane, before she had security escort me out of the clinic. "I was very clear with Dr. Smith and the recruiter about this during my interview. They did not seem to consider it an issue." "Of course they didn't" was her clipped response. She then exited her office, without a parting word or backward glance. What was I supposed to do now? What I did was spend twenty minutes fidgeting in the uncomfortable, polyester chair, debating whether I should sneak out the back entrance before anyone noticed.

Jane finally returned to her office, with an unreadable expression on her face. She informed me that Dr. Smith had confirmed my "alternative training plan" (I swear she grimaced as she said this) and that she had been instructed to escort me to my new office. As I followed her down the hall, it occurred to me that Dr. Smith had just usurped Jane's authority, which had to displease Jane, who was technically my supervisor, as the director of research at the clinic. Hmmmm. It did not take a rocket scientist to gather that that was potentially bad for me.

We entered the research office. The state of the room was shocking. Large manila folders, that resembled medical charts, covered every flat surface of the room, the desk, the sink, even the floor. Large plastic notebooks were piled high against the back wall. Mere words could not do justice to the horror I was feeling. This office was the biggest mess I had ever seen. And this was supposed to be my new work space???My expression must have struck a chord of sympathy in Jane. Her stone face softened as she attempted to explain the reason for the disaster before me. "Dr. Smith has not had a study coordinator for six weeks." She was about to provide some important details, when Dr. Smith entered the office. "Hello Lisa," she greeted me cheerfully. She then turned to Jane. "Thanks for the help. I can take it from here" were her kind, yet dismissive words. But apparently Jane was not willing to go quietly. "Dr. Smith, I don't think it's fair to schedule a monitoring visit on Lisa's first day." Dr. Smith raised her eyebrows at this declaration, clearly unaccustomed to her decisions being questioned. And for the second time, I longed to disappear into the linoleum floor.

At the excruciating, pivotal moment that Dr. Smith was going to respond to Jane, a young man entered the room. "Hi Dr. Smith. Is your new study coordinator ready to start?" were his cheerful words. However, his smile dissolved as he took note of the scene before him. The standoff between Dr. Smith and Jane stopped him dead in his tracks. He hovered uncomfortably, not sure of what to say next. This must be the monitor. Hmm.

And then I had an epiphany, a solution to the impending disaster, and a way for me to find out some important information about my job. I walked confidently across the room, hand outstretched, and introduced myself to Eric. "Hi Eric. My name is Lisa. I am Dr. Smith's new study coordinator. I know we have a lot of work to do, so let's get going." He was an obviously sharp guy; he immediately understood my intent and followed me quickly out of the research area. We kept walking until we reached the main lobby, out of ear shot.

He exhaled slowly. "Thank you for saving me from that situation. That was really uncomfortable. What was going on?" I looked up at him, and replied honestly. "I don't think Jane approves of Dr. Smith's training plan for me." Eric raised his eyebrows at this statement, but declined further comment. .

Meanwhile, I had my own set of questions for Eric. And I had already decided on full disclosure from this point forward. "Eric, do you mind telling me what a monitor is?"

# CHAPTER

3

## ARE WE THERE YET?

In the middle of a crucial conversation, my mother suddenly put me on hold. "I'll be right back" was her rushed explanation. Let me define crucial. I was very close to quitting my job, and had called my mother to hopefully talk some sense into me. Working for Dr. Smith had seemed like an exciting opportunity, but was, in reality, an impossible task. I had no idea what I was doing, and every time I turned around, another "responsibility" materialized. No human could possibly complete the enormous back log of work that was Dr. Smith's research practice.

I kept hearing my mother's voice inside my head, cautioning me against being impulsive, urging me to think things through before plunging in. Looks like she was right, again.

The telephone line clicked, and she was back. I took a deep breath and continued, "Mom, I don't think I can do this!" were my tearful, truthful words. I had worked at the clinic for less than a week and had arrived at this grim realization. It seemed as though Dr. Smith expected miracles of me, or at the very least expected me to assimilate information at lightning speed. Either expectation was impossible. I had also learned what a monitor was. Eric's basic job was to review/audit the medical data that Dr. Smith collected/reported on the patients enrolled in the drug studies she conducted, to ensure it complied with protocol requirements. The study coordinator's job was to coordinate the study, and help Dr. Smith collect, document and organize the patient data, for review and retrieval by the monitor. That included reviewing medical records, participating in patient care, drawing and processing blood, interviewing patients, creating and maintaining large amounts of paperwork, and working closely with monitors to correct/clarify data errors, on top of completing the work my predecessor had left with her mysterious departure. Eric had been tasked with teaching me how to do this job. I don't know how Dr. Smith had managed to arrange that. She was all powerful; it was better to accept this and not ask too many questions.

My crash course in clinical research started with a pneumonia study. I was tasked with reviewing binders that contained essential "regulatory" documents (the official paperwork required to start and maintain a study, as per the FDA). Institutional Review Board (IRB) study approval, the protocol, Informed Consent (ICF), 1572, financial disclosure, delegation of authority log, CVs, medical licenses, etc. These were some of the very important documents required to facilitate study conduct. Eric had me virtually memorize their content. It seemed the fate of mankind rested on this.

I then started review of the source documents, and Case Report Forms (CRFs). These were the tools used to collect and document study patient data. Source documents were the first place data was documented/collected, such as medical records, diagnostic results, x-rays, ECG reports, etc. etc. CRFs were the final place that data from the source documents was documented. CRFs were patient binders with three part carbon copy pages. The study coordinator transferred and documented data from the source documents onto the CRF pages. The monitor would review the CRFs. After final review, the monitor would retrieve the top copies of the CRF pages and send them to the pharmaceutical company sponsoring the trial.

I struggled to understand this process at this early stage, but Eric reassured me that it would all make perfect sense in time. Most importantly, it was my grave responsibility (Eric was a bit dramatic) to document study data correctly, and to ensure ALL required study procedures were completed in the required timeframe, and documented correctly. I spent hours poring through these binders. And though sometimes tedious, it was very effective and provided the best introduction to the data collection and study process.

Eric was another story. He was kind, professional, but VERY, very serious about his responsibilities. My exhausting first day continued into the evening. I left the clinic at 7pm with a reading assignment of the International Conference of Harmonization/Good Clinical Practice Guidelines (ICH/GCP), as well as the pneumonia study protocol (did I mention it was 100 pages?). Eric and I were due to start early the following morning. I was no stranger to hard work and relished a challenge. However, my brain was on information overload, and it was only the first day. I read until midnight, and awoke at 5am feeling as though I had not slept at all. But I was determined!! I showered, grabbed a protein bar, and arrived at the clinic at 7am, ready to immerse myself in microbes (a little pneumonia humor). Instead, Eric handed me an osteoarthritis protocol and instructed me to familiarize myself with the study (this protocol was 120 pages). Wait, what???

I had planned to spend the day really learning bacteria, a thorough introduction to a complex therapeutic area, not a rushed, high level summary of one complicated topic before quickly shifting to another complicated topic. "I don't understand." He ignored me and continued. "Spend an hour reading the protocol and then we can start trying to contact the lost-to-follow up patients." Lost patients? What? This was an enormously challenging educational process. Yet, I did not have a choice; I had to learn this job. So I walked to the research office to begin my reading assignment.

I was again confused by Eric's instruction. This pneumonia study had been chosen as my "introductory" study due to simple need and timing. It was the most recent study approved by the Hospital Review

Board, and still actively enrolling patients. The study with the greatest need had the greatest priority. The rest of the studies (I did not know how many there were) were on hold; their exact status had not yet been disclosed to me. How was I expected to learn a study well enough to enroll patients, when I was handed given another study to learn, and complete patient follow up? Unfortunately, this continued the entire week. I spent Tuesday morning "learning" the osteoarthritis study, and Tuesday afternoon trying to track down and convince reluctant patients (half of whom had forgotten they were still participating in the osteoarthritis study) that A: I was not a lunatic and B: That Dr. Smith needed them to return to the clinic for their final study visit, which included blood draws, physical exams and zero compensation for their time. Dr. Smith had made it very clear that there was no patient stipend in the budget. A bright spot in an otherwise difficult day was that "lost to follow up" turned out to be a straightforward research term that I quickly grasped. Patients had been participating in the study, and then when Dr. Smith's nurse quit, there hadn't been anyone to coordinate their visits and follow up. My job was to organize their final study visits and participation.

I was surprised that I was able to track down all seven patients. I was shocked when three of the seven patients agreed to return for their study visits. I attributed their agreement to two things: 1-they felt sorry for me. 2-my wonderful acting skills (when you grow up with two older brothers, you had to learn to manipulate to survive). When calling each patient, I introduced myself as Dr. Smith's new study nurse, (emphasis on "new") and pleaded with them to return to the clinic to "help Dr. Smith finish the important study." As for the remaining four patients; two calls were never returned, one patient simply hung up on me, and one patient (starving college student) refused to return unless he received a hefty stipend and mileage reimbursement. For the remaining three patients, who thankfully agreed to return, final study visits were scheduled for the following week. The visits had to be completed as soon as possible as they had been outstanding for months. . . .

I left Tuesday evening, exhausted, and with more homework. My interesting reading assignment? Why, nothing other than several chapters on the federal regulations that govern research conduct. 21 Code of Federal Regulation (CFR) parts 11, 50, and 56, electronic records, informed consent and IRB. I was up very late reading, but convinced my exhausted brain that I could handle two therapeutic areas. To my surprise, when I arrived at the clinic early Wednesday morning, Eric handed me a 130-page sinusitis protocol. A THIRD PROTOCOL!!! He instructed me to start reading it as soon as possible, as Dr. Smith needed to enroll another patient to make her enrollment quota, which ended in three weeks. But, no pressure.

I looked at Eric in shock. What kind of person expected a new employee to learn three complex therapeutic areas in three days, enroll patients on two of those studies, and perform patient follow up on the third study? He must be joking. I stared at him earnestly, waiting for the punch line, for him to laugh out loud and tell me he was kidding, that he wanted to lighten the mood. However, he had his arms folded across his chest, his face impassive, which I interpreted as "These need to be done. Please do them, and stop asking questions."

I walked slowly to my office, defeated. I tried valiantly to concentrate on the sinusitis study, but everything kept whirring around my brain like an angry hummingbird. Learning studies, enrolling patients, catching up on my workload, pleasing Dr. Smith, pleasing Eric.

The sinusitis study had some fairly complex requirements, such as cell counts, Pharmacokinetic (PK) blood testing, and Computed Tomography (CT) scans of the sinus cavity. While studying the schedule of assessments, Eric walked into my office and handed me a list of names. "We need to identify another radiologist to review CT scans for the study. Here is a list of names for you to contact." He gave me one final look and left the room, with me still holding the list, utterly dumfounded. This job was starting to feel like a bad dream.

That night, I fell asleep reviewing the sinusitis study (really, I fell asleep on top of the sinusitis study). I had several bizarre dreams that night; I presume due to sleep deprivation and stress. For example, in one dream, a mad scientist, a Dr. Frankenstein type with crazy accent and long white coat, chased me around the clinic with his otoscope, trying to look up my nose. I awoke with a start at 4 am and could not get back to sleep.

I arrived at the clinic at 8 am Thursday morning. Despite my fatigue, despite feeling overwhelmed and helpless, I was determined to see this through. If I took it one day at a time, and learned the three studies, and all of the other job requirements, I would be fine, maybe even great! And just as I was starting to feel better, I walked into my office and noticed yet another protocol on my desk. It was a 140 page document, with a yellow sticky note taped to the front cover that said "READ ME" in large black ink. I blinked again to make sure I was seeing things correctly. I unpeeled the sticky note from the protocol cover – an ankle sprain study, complete with x-rays and complicated pain assessments.

I sat at my desk, utterly speechless. Eric entered the room at the end of my long and labored sigh. "Oh hey, I was thinking we could work on the ankle sprain study today." He was all business, chipper, motivated. I was in no mood for that. I finally asked the dreaded question that had been looming in the room like the proverbial white elephant. Six simple words. "Eric, how many studies are there?" He looked me straight in the face, as he responded "five." My heart sank at his response. They expected me to learn five studies at the same time!! Eric was smart enough to leave the room when he saw how this news affected me. I felt hopeless, frustrated and really sad about everything. What a mess I had gotten myself into. And this is what led to the desperate phone call to my mother.

"Lisa, you cannot quit this job. You will never forgive yourself." I was near tears. "Mother, you have no idea what is going on here." I confessed how helpless and overwhelmed I felt. She was a wonderful listener, and provided much needed sympathy, but basically ordered me to hang in there and not give up…as if it were that easy. We spoke for several minutes and then she had to get back to work. She told me she loved me and asked me to call her later that evening. I appreciated her words, but was not particularly buoyed by the sentiment. I felt like I was failing, and that I should give up before I was fired for not being able to keep up. I laid my head in my hands and felt a tear run down my face. That was all I needed, to have Eric and Dr. Smith see me crying like a two year old. I grabbed a tissue to wipe my eyes at about the same time Eric entered the room. Someone really needed to speak to him about his bad timing.

# CHAPTER

## 4

## ARE THEY HIRING IN DERMATOLOGY?

Eric and I sat there in awkward silence. I looked out upon the piles of case report forms that covered every bare inch of space, the stacks of disorganized regulatory documents that covered the floor, patient charts piled upon sagging shelves, and I decided that I deserved an explanation for this disaster. Eric had worked alongside Dr. Smith and the other study nurse for a year. It was enough time to have gleaned a decent understanding of the situation. He seemed like a straight forward person, so I decided to ask him the question of the ages. What had caused Dr. Smith's studies to end up in such a mess?

Let me preface this by saying that even though I had only worked at the clinic for four days, in that short time, I had heard whispers, but nothing tangible, about my predecessor's sudden disappearance from the practice. She was fired, she had a mysterious illness, she had gotten married... What had happened between Dr. Smith and her prior study coordinator was veiled in mystery. Though I was naturally curious about the situation, I had decided to listen to my mother's sage advice and avoid the gossip, until now. The circumstances that had led to this moment, my frustration, the torrential state of the studies, the overwhelming work load, the rushed assimilation, had to be revealed, for I felt it would influence my decision to stay, or leave, this position.

Part of me felt it was horribly unfair that the recruiter had not told me the truth about Dr. Smith and the backlog of studies. On the other hand, I may not have taken the position, had I known the true state of things. I needed to believe that it had nothing to do with my employer, that Dr. Smith was as she seemed to me, a brilliant, demanding, kind benefactor who had taken a chance on someone with no experience. I needed to believe that she and her study coordinator had parted ways due to a personality conflict, or performance issue, and not due to an unpleasant working environment.

"Would you please tell me what happened between Dr. Smith and her coordinator?"

Eric sat down beside me. As he explained the situation, I was surprised by his candor. Apparently he also felt he had nothing to lose, except perhaps me. It seems that Dr. Smith's coordinator (let's call her "Betty") had not been completely honest about her research experience. Dr. Smith was under the impression that she had hired this highly trained study nurse to grow her clinical trials practice. Betty was a charismatic, young woman, determined to succeed in clinical research. So determined, that ambition had clouded her perception of her true skills and experience. She had convinced herself, and Dr. Smith, that she could manage a busy clinical trials practice. She had previously worked for a primary care physician, who participated in about 3-4 trials a year. She had been his study coordinator for a year and a half, before coming to work for Dr. Smith. She had persuaded everyone that she was the key to Dr. Smith's success. Her intent had not been malicious, as she really did want to succeed in the role. But the task had proven far too difficult for Betty's abilities. She had enough regulatory experience to get through study start up, but not enough long-term research experience to balance a full trial load.

Betty's outgoing personality had charmed the sponsors into bringing the studies to Dr. Smith. However, Betty's façade began to crumble as the workload grew. She started making mistakes, protocol deviations that seriously concerned Dr. Smith and her monitors. When Dr. Smith confronted Betty, there was an unpleasant exchange, and Betty basically quit before she was fired. The studies lay untouched for nearly six weeks, at the risk of irretrievable data, patients permanently lost to follow up and latent study renewal. This explained a lot, the chaos I was trying to manage, and the undertone of urgency to my learning process.

"Why didn't Dr. Smith hire anyone?" I asked. He smiled. "She tried, but nobody was the right fit, until you came along." He described a slew of candidates with the wrong kind of experience, or demeanor, for the position. "Lisa, Dr. Smith was looking for a particular candidate, honest, enthusiastic, and willing to go above and beyond to get the job done. She found that in you." I gave him a half-hearted smile. He was being very sweet, and refreshingly honest, but I was smart enough to know that he had an ulterior motive. The majority of the studies Dr. Smith conducted were sponsored by his company. It was in his and their best interests to complete them. To clean and retrieve latent study data that may ultimately delay regulatory review, if not retrieved in the next several months.

We sat in reflection for several minutes. Then Eric interrupted the silence with a question for me. "Well Lisa", Eric ventured, "what happens now?" Like most successful monitors, Eric was very intuitive and observant. He could read my frustrated body language and knew I was on the fence about this position, and a significant move from him could tip me in either direction. "Eric, this pace is ridiculous." I explained. "I don't have time to properly learn anything."

Eric knew this dilemma well. He had watched desperate investigators hire inexperienced study coordinators, with the intent of training them to conduct research the right way. With this model, a brand new study coordinator did not have to "unlearn" any bad practices...a great concept in theory. However, in practice, one needs to have time to learn and process new information, and taking over a busy research practice did not allow for that. The hectic pace, combined with the intense learning curve, led to a very high turnover rate with new study coordinators.

Eric's next words were surprising to me. "Lisa, I don't want you to quit. I know this has been hard on you. Let me talk to Dr. Smith." I shrugged my shoulders. He must have taken that gesture as an affirmative, for he smiled at me and left the room. I had nothing to lose. I didn't want to quit, but I was smart enough to know that I could not continue at this pace and do a good job. And I was not willing to take on this much responsibility, and do a mediocre job in the process of completing it. It was not my nature to do anything half-heartedly.

I spent the rest of the afternoon idly flipping through the sinusitis protocol, wondering how the day would end; with my keeping this job, under far different circumstances, or my walking away, with my integrity (and student loans) intact.

At precisely 4pm, Eric returned with Dr. Smith. I was surprised and embarrassed to see her; I had secretly hoped to avoid her, and her disappointment, throughout this conflict. Eric spoke for them both. "Dr. Smith and I realize that this may have been a bit unfair on you." I nodded and they continued. "We want you to stay." His sincere declaration had my attention. "We will give you 3 days, uninterrupted, to learn the studies. No distractions, no patients. And then we will clean up the studies together, Lisa." I thought about their proposition, the opportunity to learn this job (though it would take much longer than three days, at least I had bought myself some time), the opportunity to work with Dr. Smith, the opportunity to advance in this interesting field, and lastly, the opportunity to prove my mother wrong. Anything would be better than the last four days. I had negotiated myself a better work environment, and had perhaps gained my employer's respect in the process. "That sounds fair. Thank you for doing this for me."

Dr. Smith had been silent throughout this exchange, probably because Eric was a more down to earth sales person than the brilliant, kind, yet reticent physician who signed my paycheck. And they needed a salesman to close this proverbial deal with me. I needed to believe that they would follow through and provide me the necessary time to actually learn the studies I was expected to conduct. Eric had the enigmatic personality to provide that level of reassurance, which is what ultimately convinced me to stay.

I wanted to show my gratitude to Dr. Smith, in an appropriate manner, without making us both feel uncomfortable. Eric was approachable, Dr. Smith was not. Dr. Smith and Eric both stood to leave. "Well, then that settles it. Thanks again Lisa. We will see you tomorrow." Eric left the research office; however, Dr. Smith lingered in the doorway to speak to me. "Lisa, thank you for staying." And then she smiled, and disappeared around the corner. A woman of few, yet substantial words. I knew that once I understood her, I would learn so much from her.

I never knew exactly how Dr. Smith arranged to have Eric help train me. I figured she had arranged to hire him as a temporary contractor, from the pharmaceutical company that employed him. It really didn't matter. What did matter was that he was there enough over the next month to assist me in cleaning up his studies, while providing an adequate foundation of knowledge from which my understanding of this complex field could grow, and flourish. And thus concluded the first week of my new job.

# CHAPTER
## 5

## JUST LIKE I DID IN NURSING SCHOOL.

True to their word, the following week I was given three relatively uninterrupted days to study protocols in the following areas: pneumonia, bronchitis, sinusitis, osteoarthritis, ankle sprain and skin infection. However, it was six protocols, not five. The skin infection protocol appeared mysteriously in my in box on Monday morning. It was as if they thought I would either, A-not notice, or B-not care. I decided temporarily on both option A and B. I did not have time to learn a sixth protocol at this critical juncture. I had three days to perform a preliminary review of five studies, and additional research guidelines, so skin infections would just have to wait.

I was determined to make the most of this learning time, and modeled it after a nursing school cram session, complete with ear plugs and strong coffee. I tuned the world out as I read about pneumonia, Quality of Life Questionnaires, Placebo vs. Study Treatment, ICF process, etc. etc. Eric, of course, stopped to "check on me" several times during this time frame. He would knock quietly on the research office door, enter, and ask me how I was doing. Each time, I smiled, nodded, and continued with my reading. He eventually got the hint and left me alone the last day of this time period. I was merely taking what I was promised, the opportunity to learn, and I was going to use every minute of that opportunity.

I suspect that Dr. Smith and Eric secretly hoped that I would finish studying early, that I would miraculously process an enormous amount of information in a short amount of time, that I would be able to resume my research duties before the three days were up. They were going to be disappointed.

By Wednesday afternoon, after three full days of studying, I felt a great sense of relief. Relief about my workload, my understanding of clinical research, and about my relationship with Dr. Smith and Eric. I had reviewed a massive amount of clinical research information. Time and performance would dictate my retention of this information. I chose to focus on what I had learned, as opposed to how much more I had to learn. I now knew enough to get through most of the pending studies, with Eric's help. The rest would come.

Moments after I emerged from my proverbial cram session and opened the office door, Eric appeared. He was smiling broadly, which caused me to feel suspicious about what he and Dr. Smith had had planned for me, and then a little bit of shame over my initial suspicion. Just because I had spent three days studying difficult therapeutic indications did not mean I felt confident enough to complete skin grafts or lung biopsies. The problem was that Eric and Dr. Smith were brilliant. Brilliant people learned things quickly, and sometimes expected the people they were training to learn just as quickly. I was not close to being on their intellectual par, even on a good day, so my assimilation process would be a bit delayed in comparison.

Eric was annoyingly chipper. "How are you feeling about things?" He asked. "Very well informed." I replied sarcastically. He chose to ignore the sarcasm. "Good, because Dr. Smith wants you to start screening patients." That sounded terribly exciting to me. "Awesome" was my simple response. But it expressed the excitement I was feeling. "Great, I will let her know you are ready." And Eric was gone before I could consider the implication and possibly retract or revise my response. I may be a woman of few words today, but those few words may have gotten me into big trouble. I hope they had not lead Eric to believe that I was ready to immediately start screening study patients. . .

On the other hand, though the thought of screening a study patient daunted me, it did not make any difference. I still had to do what they wanted. I was learning what Dr. Smith expected of her staff, of her study coordinator; someone autonomous and willing to take risks. I needed to become that person.

Well, to my relief, Eric did not return with a study patient in tow. Rather, he escorted me to Dr. Smith's treatment pod to observe Dr. Smith screen a study patient.

Dr. Smith was in the middle of screening a patient for the pneumonia study. When I entered her examination room, she smiled and handed me a lab kit, with serum separator tubes, purple topped hematology tubes, blue topped clotting factor tubes, and a cup for urine collection. A smart move to build my confidence. Dr. Smith knew I had a strong lab background and could literally draw blood in my sleep. Without hesitation, I washed my hands, donned a pair of latex gloves and grabbed a tourniquet. The patient had excellent veins, and I drew the study blood tests effortlessly. Dr. Smith asked me to label and process them immediately, and I felt exhilarated as I walked the blood samples over to our makeshift lab area. I had just completed my first study assessment. And that is how I spent the next week, observing Dr. Smith screen study patients, while completing additional screening procedures relative to each study protocol. This included drawing PK specimens, completing urine pregnancy tests, taking vital signs, completing ECGs, and obtaining patient diaries and questionnaires. It was an organized and methodical way to allow me to participate in and learn the study patient screening process.

My training with Eric continued through the next week, and for several monitoring visits over the next month. I developed a theory as to how Dr. Smith arranged to have a monitor train her new study coordinator, which was a highly uncommon occurrence. Dr. Smith was a very important investigator to this particular sponsor. She was motivated, involved and a high enroller on studies. As previously mentioned, Eric's company had a vested interest in bringing the neglected studies to full course. They needed the clinical trials data to support pending drug applications. Eric's training would expedite the data retrieval process, not to mention teaching me the correct way to obtain data. It was as simple as that. Eric's mundane reading assignments provided the theoretical content of my training. However, the practical application of my training (patient interaction and study procedures, such as drawing blood, obtaining specimens, completing source documents and CRFs) is where I really learned to be a study coordinator.

# CHAPTER

## 6

## ABOUT THAT SPUTUM SAMPLE.

One Friday, about three weeks into my employment, I completed my first study patient screening visit. It was an unexpected, highly important and slightly hilarious moment. It had been a quiet morning, so I took advantage of the unexpected lull to review the visit schedule for our active pneumonia study. I was leaning back in my chair, intently studying the schedule of events, when Dr. Smith suddenly appeared. I was so deep in concentration that I did not hear her approach. When she started speaking, it startled me, which caused me to jump in my seat and knock the chair to the floor, with me in it. It was like a scene from a bad B movie, papers flying everywhere, me prone on the floor with the concerned face of my employer hovering anxiously above. "Lisa, are you ok?"

This was not the way I imagined impressing Dr. Smith, with my confidence and efficiency; her pulling me slowly off of the floor while I wiped dust and staples off of my lab coat. Once upright, I felt a little sheepish and a lot embarrassed. "Um," was all I could muster. But Dr. Smith was having none of my awkwardness. The next words out of her mouth caught me completely by surprise. Smiling (broadly), speaking (effusively), she informed me that she had found a possible pneumonia patient for me to screen. "What?" I said in complete surprise. She nodded quickly. "WE need to move fast, so let's go." I paused for a brief moment. Dr. Smith felt I was ready to screen my first study patient. And then it hit me. DR SMITH FELT I WAS READY TO SCREEN MY FIRST STUDY PATIENT!! This was awesome; this was terrifying; and this was really happening! I turned around to grab lab kits and source documents for the screening visit, chattering about various items we would need for the screening. When I turned back around, Dr. Smith was already gone. Naturally, anything except top speed was to slow for her. I rolled my eyes (couldn't resist), grabbed my supplies and raced out the door to her pod of examination rooms.

Moments later I arrived, breathless and perspiring from excitement and exertion. Dr. Smith, poised like a wax statue, took note of my appearance and frowned slightly. What did she expect? I wasn't a super hero like her. I breathed and sweated like a normal human. She handed me a handkerchief from her lab coat pocket, to mop my brow. And then understanding hit me. It does not lend reassurance to a nervous study patient when the person collecting blood and body fluids for analysis was sweaty and breathless!

I wiped my brow, collected myself, and we walked into the examination room. There was an elderly gentleman seated on the examination table. She clasped his hand, and it was clear he was besotted with his physician, as there was absolute adoration and trust on his face as he smiled up at her. Dr. Smith appropriately reciprocated by asking about his grandkids, his wife and his last fishing trip. Her recall of each patient's medical and personal history was startling; it was one of the many reasons Dr. Smith had such a successful medical practice. She made her patients feel important with her manner of attention and individualized care.

They spoke for a few more minutes, and then Dr. Smith introduced me to the patient. She explained that I would be collecting blood and sputum to test for the pneumonia study. He smiled and shook my hand. His grasp felt cold and unsteady, displaying age? Nerves? For all this patient knew, I was an experienced study coordinator. I wanted him to feel comfortable, and so I willed myself to remain calm and focused throughout the process.

Dr. Smith had already explained the study and all requirements to the patient; she had obtained his consent earlier that day. She thankfully insisted that I was not yet ready to independently consent a study patient. It was a critical process that required time and consideration, and she would not rush that component of my training. It was too important for me to learn how to correctly consent a study patient. Dr. Smith reviewed the screening requirements with the patient again, the process for blood and sputum collection, the paperwork to complete, and the expected timeframe for eligibility consideration. She wanted to ensure his full understanding. She reminded him that it was his right to discontinue study treatment at any time, without recrimination, and that he would be given the approved treatment for his illness. His reply to her repeated explanation was comical. "Dr. Smith, I get it. I am not your guinea pig. Your gal and I will be fine. You can leave us to our studying." I pursed my lips to stifle a giggle. A complicated clinical discussion was made simple by an elderly gentleman in cataract sun- glasses and polyester pants. Gotta love that! Dr. Smith gave her patient a brief hug, and exited the room. I took a deep breath. Oh boy, here I go.

I needed to obtain the central lab blood tests first, to allow for adequate clotting of blood before processing, so I started organizing the lab kits on the tray next to the examination table. I chatted briefly with the patient while I performed this task. Suddenly, without provocation, the patient started hacking. It was a deep, wet, chest cough that made me wince. The cough was so strong that his face was turning red with exertion. I felt faint stirrings of nausea and experienced a nursing school flashback. My kryptonite, the only thing in patient care that made me ill, was sputum; a green, gooey, disgusting substance that made me vomit every time. In nursing school we completed a rotation at a skilled nursing facility with ventilator patients. Tracheas overrun with secretions and patients that gurgled as they struggled to breathe greeted me at every turn. I began to detest anything sputum related, and would negotiate terms with my fellow classmates in an attempt to avoid dealing with sputum. I would change their patient's bedpans or help them write term papers, in exchange for suctioning tracheas.

Don't get me wrong, I took my responsibilities as a nurse very seriously. I only delegated the respirator care of patients to my classmates. I dutifully completed the rest of their care. My aversion to sputum, and what I was willing to do to avoid it, amused my classmates. I made it through the rest of that particular nursing rotation negotiating terms of avoidance quite successfully. It was poetic justice that I now found myself face-to-face with my nemesis, phlegm. Only I could not barter my way out of this one. This patient sounded like he had the perfect specimen to provide. And it was not going to collect itself.

Resigned, I grabbed the lab kit from the bedside and asked the patient to try and produce a specimen for me. He nodded as I handed him the sterile container. I started to explain the process to ensure an accurate collection when he cleared his throat and spit something thick into the sterile container provided. He smiled triumphantly and handed it to me. I glimpsed the green mess and felt my eyes begin to water. That was followed by a cold sweat and a sudden onslaught of nausea. Moving quickly, I informed the patient that I needed to quickly refrigerate (what?) the specimen, and that I would return in a few minutes. He nodded as I excused myself from the room.

I raced down the hallway towards the research area. I dumped the specimen on the counter top in the lab area, and literally ran to the employee locker room. I splashed cold water on my face, and thought of unicorns and dandelions, anything to clear my head and not throw up. This may have seemed silly, but we all have our weaknesses. I stared at my dripping reflection in the mirror and couldn't help but smile. I didn't throw up. That was an amazing first when dealing with phlegm. I may not have conquered my revulsion, but I had successfully dealt with it, which would make subsequent sample collection much easier. I dried my face and returned to the examination room. I thanked the patient for providing an awesome specimen for analysis. Dr. Smith would be pleased, and I would be forgiven for the white lie I told the patient about his sputum to avoid an embarrassing scene. I drew the patient's blood for testing and completed the screening visit paperwork. I then escorted the patient to the scheduler's desk to coordinate the study chest x-ray. The last piece of the puzzle. If the chest x-ray showed an effusion or infiltrate, we could have our first study patient. I thanked the patient sincerely for his cooperation, which had helped me immensely through the complicated screening process.

When I finally returned to the research area with the paperwork and blood specimens, Dr. Smith was waiting for me. She inquired as to the visit status, and I proudly informed her that it had gone without incident. She smiled and congratulated me on a job well done. I was glad to see her for the next steps were not clear to me, specifically, processing the sputum sample. It required a laboratory gram stain, and I needed direction as to the process of testing with our hospital lab.

And here is where the fun began. Dr. Smith explained that she did not contract with the hospital lab for the study gram stains, due to their high costs. She had instead arranged for the hospital lab technician to train me how to complete a gram stain on the sputum specimen. I was amenable to this, having spent several years as a hospital phlebotomist while working my way through nursing school. For once with this job, an environment NOT foreign to me. The blessed, glorious lab! Dr. Smith instructed me to ask for the lead technician at the lab to facilitate the training, and then rushed off to her afternoon clinic. I was looking forward to meeting the unfortunate lab technician Dr. Smith had charmed into teaching me the art of gram stains. Little did I know that he would not exactly be pleased to have been selected as my instructor.

# CHAPTER

# 7

# IT DOES NOT PERMANENTLY STAIN!

The hospital lab was located on the basement level, down the hall from the hospital cafeteria. The location choice puzzled me. Lab staff were plating and growing bacteria in an area not far from where people were eating the tuna special. It was speculated that the tuna special was so bad that it had to have been grown in the lab. And that was my ridiculous thought process as I walked into the laboratory waiting area (random thought storm hit whenever I felt nervous).

There was a young woman seated at the lab front desk, absorbed in her smart phone. I walked right up to her, and she kept right on texting without acknowledging me. After several awkward moments, (she was either oblivious or very rude) I decided to interrupt her texting session. "Hello." No response. I tried again. I cleared my throat, cracked my knuckles, and decided to speak a full sentence for effect. 'Um, can you help me?' She finally looked up from her very important texting session, and narrowed her eyes at me. Someone was not amused. Good thing that did not bother me. I introduced myself as Dr. Smith's research nurse and asked to speak with the lead lab technician. "What is this regarding?" was her token response. I explained that Dr. Smith had arranged for the technician to train me on gram stains. This elicited zero response from her. "Maybe you could go get him?" I ventured. She sighed dramatically, rose from her chair (round one, me) and walked to the back lab area to fetch the technician. I had a sinking feeling that this was not going to be as effortless as Dr. Smith had assured me.

After nearly fifteen minutes, a very pale, very thin, very 'sciencey' looking individual (receding hairline, lab coat, pencil pocket protector) came out to the waiting area, following by the texting receptionist (who was now smirking at me). The look on his face was not that of a helpful mentor. I smiled and tried to introduce myself, but was stopped short by a dismissive wave of his hand. "I know who you are and like I told Dr. Smith, I don't have time to teach you how to do gram stains. I can give you some materials to practice with, but that is the best I can do!" he curtly informed me. I physically willed myself to vanish into the linoleum floor as he continued his tirade about 'spoiled physicians' with "unrealistic expectations of their subordinates." He then motioned for me to follow him to the back lab area.

We made our way past ominous lab testing equipment, countless rows of beakers, microscopes and centrifuges. Lab personnel, with safety visors and goggles, were poised above stainless steel and electronic devices, testing every body fluid known to man. The lab was enormous. We kept walking until we reached a large sink area at the back of the lab. There were several bottles of purple dye and agar plates piled two feet high. On the wall above the sink, very simple instructions were posted on a word document. "How to complete a gram stain" in bold font. It was a bulleted instruction list of how to, literally, complete a gram stain. I wonder if the technician had quickly typed it up in the fifteen-minute time period I had been forced to wait for him, so remedial was the content. Step 1, step 2, etc., etc. So this was Dr. Smith's idea of "being trained" by the lab technician?

"Here is where you work," he announced. I looked at him, then at the ridiculous piece of paper on the wall that was my only training tool, and then back at him in disbelief. Are you kidding me??? I wanted to scream at him, but instead, I barely managed a pitiful sigh. His eyes met mine. If the eyes were the window to the soul, then mine were a veritable neon sign of distress and confusion. His eyes showed pure annoyance… none of the sympathy I had hoped for. He shrugged his shoulders and turned to leave. His parting words to me? "Make sure you clean up after yourself." And then he was gone.

I sat there for a few moments, not knowing whether to laugh or cry. I ran my hands through my hair, and signed deeply. How was I going to train myself to complete gram stains like this??!! Think Lisa think. What is the next best step? But my traitorous mind remained blank. Argh!! Should I call Dr. Smith? Should I go back to my office and ask Jane to help me?

And then, FINALLY, a plan formulated, a mediocre plan borne of pure necessity, and zero alternative. I had no other choice. I had to follow the ridiculous instructions and teach myself how to gram stain. I was certainly not going to cry to Dr. Smith, or cow in defeat to Jane. I vowed that I would not leave the lab until I had completed one decent gram stain. So did that mean that I would spend the weekend behind the microbiology plates? Would anyone even miss me? Would they send a search party and find me buried underneath a monstrous pile of sputum and purple dye? My only comfort was this latent tenacity that had developed in me over the last week; I had been forced to figure so many things on my own that I was sure I would never have to ask for any kind of assistance ever again. And so I began.

The directions posted above the sink made the process seem fairly simple. It seems you took said sputum sample, spread it across the "plate", soaked it with the purple dye, and let it dry. Lather, rinse, repeat. Easy peasy. I looked around to make sure no one was watching my pathetic attempts, and then I went for it. . First and foremost, I donned my latex gloves. I then grabbed the face mask I had purchased on line to deal with any more sudden sputum encounters. Finally, holding my breath, I opened the sterile container of sputum. The sample was a thick, green, gooey mess, and I desperately wished I could close my eyes. The swab entered the viscous sample and I made sure the amount obtained was sufficient for plating. I then slowly covered the plate with a layer of the sputum, placed it on the counter top and put the sterile container to the side. Steps one and two complete. I then began the third step, the application of the dye. Those bottles were filled with that purple liquid that I am sure would permanently stain. How could I lightly saturate a plate with a bottle of that size? What to do, what to do?

It was then that I noticed a smaller plastic bottle adjacent to the sink. It was topped by a thin, straw like plastic tube, and looked perfect for producing a smaller stream of dye to accommodate the plating. I deftly transferred a small amount of purple dye from the large to the smaller container. I then lifted the smaller dye bottle, and positioned it above the plated sputum, for the most direct stream line. I squeezed the bottle in what I considered a gentle manner. Unfortunately, I did not gauge my grasp correctly. A perfect arc of purple dye danced into the air much as I imagined the water cascaded at a Las Vegas fountain show. As elegant as the ascent, the descent was merciless and produced a perfect splash of purple dye that decorated my scrubs, the sink, the counter top, every visible area except the plate. A second aim and squeeze brought similar but farther reaching results; it hit the left wall adjacent to the sink area and was dripping down the wall in the manner of an art exhibit gone awry. NO NO NO!! I whispered harshly to no one in particular. This was not going quite as I had planned.

As I attempted a third squeeze, a gloved hand intercepted my attempt and grabbed the spray bottle completely out of my hand. The technician that had abandoned me in this location had apparently come to save me, or save any uncovered counter top from my lethal aim. He looked at the purple mess I had made of his precious lab area, and instead of the anticipated tongue lashing, he started to smile. The smile turned into a roar of laughter, complete with gasps, snorts and the proverbial watering of eyes. At the conclusion of this hilarity, with two swipes of his gloved hands he perfectly plated and stained two sputum samples for me. My eyes were wide with surprise and gratitude as he handed them to me for transport. He even stayed to monitor my next several attempts, which thankfully concluded with two successfully stained plates.

I was so grateful for his assistance and thanked him profusely. Again, he waved his hand, but in a gesture of acknowledgement vs. dismissal. He also apologized for his previous behavior. "Look," he began. "I did not mean to be rude. You are not the first nurse Dr. Smith has sent down here to learn about gram stains. We are short staffed and I would have appreciated advance notice. It isn't personal." I just smiled back at him in understanding. We both knew Dr. Smith's "style." It was to presume that her way was "the way", sometimes to the inconvenience of others, though her intent was never malicious. Her intent was for me to learn and, by gosh, did I ever!! Though it may have been preliminarily uncomfortable, I could not protest, for the end result was me learning yet another crucial task, not to mention saving the ever important budget. I looked around the absolutely horrific, purple mess I had made, and started to apologize. The lab technician smiled again, and informed me that the house keepers would clean this up in no time. He then gestured towards my stained lab coat and scrubs. To my horror, I was covered from neckline to seam in zig-zagging lines of the purple dye; my coat and scrubs were ruined and I did not have a replacement set upstairs. I resembled a certain cartoon dinosaur that will remain nameless. It was pathetic and hysterical at the same time.

I paused for a moment. I would be walking up stairs, triumphant, with the necessary specimen to finishing screening my first study patient. I had learned to complete a decent enough gram stain that we did not have to worry about ancillary lab costs or bypassing potential patients due to my lack of knowledge. In the big picture, spending the day resembling said dinosaur was a harmless option compared to the alternative, telling Dr. Smith I did not successfully learn the art of gram staining. I shrugged my shoulders, as that was not my imminent concern, and there was nothing I could do about it anyway. I gave him a farewell smile, a final thank you, and made my way to the medical arts building elevators. I tried to ignore the strange looks I received from my fellow hospital employees. My goal of the day was to avoid Dr. Smith until I could find a large enough lab coat to cover the purple explosion that was my uniform. I would then triumphantly present her with the gram stain she had requested.

# CHAPTER

# 8

## I WOULD NOT MAKE A GOOD SPY.

I managed to sneak back to the research area, deposit the gram stains on the processing table, and make a break for the employee locker room, unnoticed. Or so I thought. As I stealthily approached the sink to start the laborious cleaning process (of my lab coat and clothes), Dr. Smith's secretary entered the rest room. I caught her look of surprise (and disgust) as she took in my appearance. She shook her head slowly. "Do I even want to know what happened?" As she did not have a clinical background, and even less patience for nonsense, I provided an explanation that she could accept. I informed that I had just finished a complicated research procedure for Dr. Smith. She took in my crazy purple appearance and nodded in understanding. She had worked for Dr. Smith for over ten years, and was accustomed to the strange happenings in the research department. She had learned that it was best not ask a lot of questions and accept the weirdness.

I asked if she had seen Dr. Smith. She confirmed that Dr. Smith was at a lunch meeting, and would return in about an hour and a half. Translation: "You have ninety minutes to clean yourself up and look like a human." I thanked her again, and she left me to my clean-up regimen. I scrubbed my arms, hands, face, neck, e.g. all areas affected by the purple ink blast. I managed to clean off most of the gram stain ink, with the exception of my cuticle and nail area. That would not draw suspicion as those were areas routinely affected when completing gram stains. However, my disastrous scrubs were another story. I did not have a spare pair to change into, and my second lab coat was on back order. After ten minutes of searching through empty lockers, I happened upon an extra-large lab coat hanging in an unclaimed locker. Though enormous, (I had gone from resembling the dinosaur, to another famous car tire character) it disguised the mess of my scrubs and would have to suffice. I could craft an explanation for my appearance later. Now I needed to process and ship the gram stains for confirmatory testing at the central lab.

As I walked back to the research area, Jane approached me. "How are things going?" she asked innocently enough, but I knew better. Jane knew exactly what was going on in clinical research, at all times. I was convinced she had a network of spies, and felt sure she had heard of my adventures in the lab. I never quite trusted her motives. One minute she was all helpful assistance; the next she was uncooperative resistance. That did not stop me from sharing the news of my first screening visit with her. "I just taught myself how to complete a gram stain!" I exclaimed. She raised her eyebrows in surprise. "Good for you. You are the first." She took in the change in lab coat, the purple cuticles, and smiled in appreciation. "I know that wasn't easy. You should be proud of yourself."

We continued chatting until we reached the research area. She stood in the corner as I grabbed a lab requisition slip and started to process the specimens for shipment. "You know, you can do gram stains in the employee bathroom down the hall." She informed me. I looked up at her in surprise. She continued. "I know the lab staff are less than helpful, and it would save you time and hassle." I considered her option. Not having to deal with sarcastic reception staff, harried lab technicians, and trudging down to the basement every time we needed a gram stain seemed like a dream come true. "That is so great.

You are sure that it won't be a problem?" She smiled sweetly and informed me that it shouldn't be a problem at all. She then looked down at her watch and raced for the door. Apparently she was late for some meeting. Her parting words for me were "just don't forget to clean up." I considered her words helpful, but I should have paid more attention to them. And I should have known better than to accept her kindness without question.

After the specimens had been processed and packaged for the central lab, I called back down to the lab for gram stain supplies. When the lab technician learned I would no longer need to destroy his sink for the purposes of Dr. Smith's research, he was more than happy to provide a lifetime supply of gram stain supplies. The lab courier arrived thirty minutes later with bags of swabs, plates, and four bottles of the infamous purple dye. After organizing everything in the research area, I noticed that I had thirty minutes to spare until my next patient visit. A perfect opportunity to practice gram stains in my new laboratory, e.g. the employee bathroom. I needed to familiarize with the space and perfect my staining technique.

It was early Monday afternoon, and Dr. Smith had finished seeing patients. Her partner was on holiday and the area was virtually deserted. It seemed safe enough to practice. I grabbed all necessary supplies and headed off to my makeshift "laboratory." The bathroom was surprisingly small and personal looking for an "employee" rest room. Sink, toilet, potted plant and generic Monet print hanging from the wall. It was the strangest employee restroom I had ever seen. However, I was not about to question Jane's offer, which almost seemed too good to be true. Now was the time to focus and practice. I swabbed a plate with water, and sprayed the plate with the purple dye, attempting to repeat the technique demonstrated by the lab technician. My traitorous arm was unfortunately not steady, and once again I decorated my surroundings with the purple dye. Wall, sink, toilet. Only this time it was not such a problem. I had the necessary supplies to clean my practice area of all signs of gram stain dye, courtesy of the lab technician's instruction, and the nearby janitor's closet. I continued to stain plates until I felt more confident with my technique. The bathroom was another story. The mess was horrific; it was not going to clean itself. My plan was to take the gram stain accessories back to the research area, and stop by the janitor's closet for the cleaning supplies, on my way back to the employee restroom. After I deposited my makeshift "specimens" in the research area, I grabbed detergent and scrub brushes from the janitor's closet, and headed back the employee bathroom. To my surprise, the bathroom door was locked, which meant it was occupied. This was not good. The purpose of the employee bathroom was for staff to avoid the inconvenience and mess of the patient restrooms. The individual currently using this rest room was getting much worse than the typical bathroom mess.

I waited outside of the bathroom until the person was finished. I needed to apologize and explain the strange mess. When the door opened, I was horrified at who appeared. It was none other than the director of the internal medicine clinic, Dr. Janice Walker. She was only a world famous physician, who made infrequent visits to her office in between speaking tours and educational conferences. Early on, she had been identified to me as someone to try to impress and never annoy. She was brilliant and impatient, with low tolerance for fools. And from the way she glared down at me from her imposing height, I was clearly the fool of the floor.

She took note of the bucket of cleaning supplies at my feet and probably thought I was a negligent housekeeper, not an overly enthusiastic study nurse. But how could I explain that to someone like her? I attempted an apology. "Dr. Walker, I am so sorry, I was just coming back to clean up and did not think anyone would be using the bathroom." She put her hands on her hips and literally shook her index finger in my face. "When you use my bathroom for your little experiments, make sure you clean up after yourself!" And she gave me one final withering look, before storming back to her office. My face felt hot with embarrassment. I leaned against the stainless steel wall, drained from the events of the day. I had been caught creating mock gram stains in the personal bathroom of the clinic medical director. And I was still alive and not prohibited from further use. But Jane had told me it was the employee bathroom. I was confused by these events. Would Jane deliberately mislead me about the use of the director's bathroom in an attempt to exact some petty revenge against Dr. Smith? Or did she truly think that it would not be a problem, with the infrequency of Dr. Walker's clinic visits? I pondered this as I scrubbed the bathroom sink. Two years of nursing school and thousands of dollars of debt accrued for what? I was scrubbing bathrooms, playing in mucous and annoying prominent physicians. It felt like high school microbiology all over again. I just hoped the chief of surgery didn't share this bathroom with Dr. Walker, because then I was in real trouble.

# THE FIRST INFORMED CONSENT
# DISCUSSION.

About five weeks into my new position, I consented my first study patient. It was an experience I will never forget. In truth, I was entrusted with this responsibility a little prematurely. However, my comprehensive training ensured a positive outcome. It is critical for the individual obtaining consent to fully understand the process, for it is far more than a permission slip that explains a common medical procedure. It is the means by which a patient is informed of the entire study process, study procedures, study medication, and more importantly, their rights and responsibilities as study patients. It must be explained by an individual with both medical and research training, to avoid possible injury to the patient with an insufficient or incorrect explanation of the study and investigational drug treatment. My first informed consent discussion embodied the importance of a detailed discussion and prevented a possibly negative outcome.

Dr. Smith personally trained me on informed consent process and conduct. She reiterated the importance of a patient's full understanding of the informed consent and overall study. She continually stressed how crucial it was for a patient to make an unbiased decision to enroll in a clinical trial, based on what he/she decide is in his/her best interests, with the full information provided. It is far too complex a process to address with simple "yes or no" mindset. She explained why the ICF is purposefully detailed, to be reviewed, considered, dissected, discussed with family, physician, and then reviewed again before a decision is made to participate in the study. A steadfast and stern responsibility, to both the individual obtaining informed consent, and the study patient signing the informed consent. Much to my good fortune, the first patient I consented was extremely bright, and very much an active participant in her health treatment. She paid close attention to every sentence of the ICF I reviewed. It would have come to a potentially bad conclusion, otherwise.

On Tuesday afternoon, Dr. Smith came down to the research office and informed me that we finally had a potential patient for our very challenging, very slow enrolling ankle sprain study. She was smiling in triumph, and I felt immediate relief. Despite rigorous effort, we had been unsuccessful in recruiting patients for the study due to very stringent eligibility criteria. We had plenty of screen failures, but not one tangible patient until now. This was the first patient to come from a direct ER referral, which increased the potential for study inclusion and was the reason for our shared enthusiasm.

Dr. Smith directed me to the screening materials and informed consent. Together we walked at a reasonable pace (at last) to her pod of examination rooms. This was such an important learning opportunity for me, to observe Dr. Smith conduct the full informed consent process. Due to her schedule, and the fragmented circumstances of study patient identification, I had only been able to observe portions of the informed consent process.

Dr. Smith knocked gently on the examination room door. A pleasant voice gave us permission to enter; the door opened to an attractive, middle aged woman with her left leg encased in a plaster cast and moon boot. After the requisite introductions, she told us of her injury. She had been standing on a rickety ladder in the garage, reaching for a suitcase stored high on a shelf, when the ladder collapsed. The resulting fall caused a left ankle sprain. The patient was admitted to the ER at 10am, and was sitting in our exam room three hours later. A master strategist, Dr. Smith had placed several of the ankle sprain study posters (IRB approved) in the nursing station of the ER, and had discussed the study at length with several ER physicians. The physicians in turn discussed the study with the ER staff. As a result of Dr. Smith's marketing efforts, an ER nurse thought of the study when the patient was first admitted, and the rest is history. Trust me, that lucky nurse would have some type of goody basket at her working pod before the evening was over. Dr. Smith gave recognition where it was due, and saw the opportunity to gain an ally in nearly every encounter.

Dr. Smith sat in an exam chair and explained the basic elements of the study to the patient. This was the patient's first "high level" introduction to the study, and opportunity to decide if she wanted to hear more, or completely decline the research opportunity and receive traditional treatment for the accident. The patient asked for more information; thus Dr. Smith began the full explanation of the study informed consent. Design, objectives, eligibility, study timeframe, and patient responsibilities were all reviewed in great detail with the patient. Dr. Smith reminded the patient that she could withdraw consent from the study at any time, without consequence, and that she would be provided with full treatment for her illness. Dr. Smith reminded the patient of her rights, and responsibilities as a study patient. The patient nodded gravely throughout the conversation. It was apparent that she both understood and respected the importance of this process, and would not make a decision lightly.

Dr. Smith gave the patient a pen, some paper, and an informed consent form. She asked the patient to review the consent and to write down any questions about the study. After informing the patient that we would return in about an hour to check her progress, we exited the examination room. The patient was thoughtful and intelligent. I hoped she would consent to participate in the study.

Dr. Smith's cell phone started ringing as soon as we closed the examination room door. When she glanced at the caller ID, her expression became serious and she excused herself to take the call. On the surface, there was nothing strange about this. Dr. Smith had her private practice, research practice, and sat on several hospital boards. She was extremely busy, and spent a lot of time fielding telephone calls. But when several more minutes passed, I began to get worried. Dr. Smith's typical phone conversation lasted less than three minutes; she was forced to be an efficient multi-tasker, due to her hectic schedule. I often joked that she could complete a major medical procedure while composing a grocery list and rocking her 3-year-old to sleep at the same time. The length of this particular call was very atypical.

Several minutes later, Dr. Smith rounded the corner with a concerned expression on her face. She explained the situation to me. One of her elderly patients had been admitted to the ER for a stroke, and she needed to attend the admission process. I dreaded her next words. "I cannot finish consenting the patient right now, Lisa." I nodded in understanding, and she continued. "I feel very comfortable with your finishing the discussion and obtaining consent. However, if you are not comfortable, we can stop right here." She looked directly into my eyes. "I know you can do this, but I don't want you to feel pressured. WE can always find another patient." I trusted Dr. Smith's sincerity about this. She would not have me complete this important of a task if I felt any hesitation, not with the gravity of obtaining informed consent. It required confidence, competence and laser focus.

I didn't even have to consider my answer. Dr. Smith had painstakingly trained me on every step of the informed consent process. I may feel a little nervous regarding the circumstances, as I always thought she would be there when I signed my first consent form. However, I wanted to show her that I was capable, that I could complete this independently. This would validate her training, and her investment in my career development. "Dr. Smith, please go attend to your patient. I can consent the patient." She smiled at my decision. "I knew you could do this." Before she left, she instructed me to review every page of the ICF with the patient and to write down any questions the patient had, that I could not answer. She reminded me to find Dr. Jones, the Sub I, if there were any issues during the informed consent discussion. If the patient felt the least uncomfortable, I was to cancel the ICF process and escort the patient to orthopedics for treatment.

I sat down on a bench outside of the examination room, and reviewed the ICF training steps that Dr. Smith had pounded into my brain. If I trusted the information, and trusted my training, things would turn out well for everyone participating. Whether the patient qualified for the study or not.

About twenty-five minutes later, the patient opened the examination room door and informed me that she had finished reading the consent form. We normally give patients forty-five minutes to an hour for the ICF review, so I felt comfortable with the time she had spent reading the document. I confess to feeling nervous about starting this important discussion with the patient. But, regardless of how I felt internally, I needed to present an external picture of compassion and composure to the patient during this discussion. I entered the examination room and sat on a chair opposite the patient. I took a deep breath, and started reading the first paragraph of the informed consent. Dr. Smith required all individuals to whom she delegated the responsibility of informed consent, to review every single page of the informed consent with the study patient, after her initial review. After I reviewed each page, the patient initialed at the bottom. The patient was very engaged in the discussion, and asked appropriate questions. Things were going well. That is, until we reached the section on study exclusion criteria. Exclusion criteria #3 was specific to cardiac history and conditions. When I started reviewing this, the patient's demeanor changed. She asked me to repeat it again. I reviewed the list of exclusionary cardiac conditions, and the patient shook her head in dismay. She had recently been diagnosed with mitral valve prolapse, and though not a specifically listed condition on the exclusion list, it was enough of a worry to cause her to decide against study participation. The patient started to apologize to me, and I stopped her immediately. "It is your right to say no to us." I reassured her. "I am thankful that you paid such close attention to what I was reading. We would never want you to regret such an important decision."

I took a deep breath and closed the ICF, thankful for the enlightened and thorough training I had received. Though we were not sure if the study drug would affect or interfere with the patient's condition, one did not enter a clinical trial with fear of risk. The patient was smart enough to put her health first, and we were educated enough to respect her decision to decline the study and seek alternative treatment. It was her right, and it was our responsibility. A better learning experience could not have been provided.

# CHAPTER
## 10

## I GUESS I AM OK WITHOUT YOU
## (NOT REALLY).

Early Monday morning, Dr. Smith came to my office, visibly distressed. She had an unexpected family emergency and would be out of the office for the remainder of the week. She informed me that Dr. Jones, our sub investigator, would be providing emergency coverage for our study patients in her absence. I held back any questions I had about her family issues. She was clearly upset, and I did not want to add to her stress level with my curiosity (of course I was dying to know what was going on). So I listened to her instruction, and reassured her that we would take care of things while she was gone. "We will be fine here. Please just take care of your family, and know that we are thinking of you." She gave me a thankful smile and reminded me to call her if I needed anything. And with that she was gone.

I felt a combination of concern and unease with Dr. Smith's unfortunate news. Concern for her well-being, and unease with her absence from the clinic for an entire week. This was the first time I would truly be "on my own" here. For even though my duties did not always require Dr. Smith's participation, they always included her collaboration. Just knowing that she was on the same hospital campus, and thus reachable, lent a level of reassurance that helped me through the most challenging tasks.

I thought of my alternatives to Dr. Smith. Dr. Jones, though a brilliant physician, was a begrudging sub investigator, and had promised his assistance in the event of an emergency or unscheduled patient visit. Nothing more. And Jane? She hovered in the periphery, to ensure her beloved department did not implode with some error I committed. She was, otherwise, not any help. I sighed deeply and prayed for an uneventful week.

I spent the morning trying to catch up on paperwork and administrative tasks. But, I found it difficult to concentrate and did not accomplish much. I kept thinking about Dr. Smith, her family, Dr. Jones covering a patient emergency, etc. Right before lunch, Dr. Smith's nurse, Jenna, made a rare appearance in my office. She had several letters in her hand. "These came in the mail Friday afternoon. They have nothing to do with the practice, so I assumed you would know what to do with them." I looked up at her, barely acknowledging the letters. White envelopes with small writing that meant nothing to me. I had no clue what they were. Dr. Smith had not provided any instruction regarding her correspondence while she was gone. I was already feeling overwhelmed with my workload; I did not have time to decide if I should read Dr. Smith's private mail and the possible negative ramifications if I made the mistake of doing so against her wishes. The letters would have to wait until her return next week.

Jenna's request had interrupted my already-burgeoning workload, and I am afraid my reply indicated my annoyance. "She didn't tell me anything about her mail. I have no idea what they are for," I brusquely informed her. Jenna's eyes narrowed at my terse reply. She turned sharply and walked away, without a response. I instantly regretted my words. We were obviously both worried about Dr. Smith and the unknown. But I felt especially bad for Jenna. She and Dr. Smith had worked together for eleven years and had a very close relationship. It had been a difficult transition for Jenna to share her employer with the likes of me. At best, Jenna viewed me as an interloper who interfered with Dr. Smith's patient care with my sputum samples and investigational drug nonsense. She did not understand, nor care much, for the entire research enterprise. However, despite her personal feelings, she was always helpful when I needed her to fit a research patient into Dr. Smith's practice schedule, or request medical records to confirm a diagnosis. I owed her the same kindness, as well as a big apology.

I walked slowly down the hall towards Dr. Smith's treatment pod. Jenna sat at her desk, staring blankly at her computer screen. She did not acknowledge my presence. "Jenna, I am sorry. I know you are worried about Dr. Smith, and I appreciate your bringing the letters. I think you are right and that I should look at them. Would you mind giving them to me?" She turned slowly and looked at me. "I brought you the letters because they looked important." I nodded in understanding. Though she was not smiling, she was no longer glaring at me. I had won a small battle. I would work on the war later. She made a better ally than enemy.

Jenna had placed the letters on Dr. Smith's desk. I looked closer and saw that they were from the diagnostic lab utilized for our pneumonia study. I opened them slowly. One was a lab report for one of our study patients, with extremely high liver enzyme results that had CLINICALLY SIGNIFICANT in red font next to the abnormal readings. Dr. Smith was on an airplane headed to God knows where, and these results were two days old. I knew instinctively to call Dr. Jones. Liver enzymes elevated to five times the upper limit of normal warranted medical attention. And for the first time in years, the physician following up on a study patient was not Dr. Smith. Dr. Smith took the term "investigator oversight" very seriously. She was very involved in our clinical trials, and treated every study patient personally. She was reluctant to delegate any physician required duties, unlike other research physicians. Her dedication contributed to our high patient retention rate, and overall success in studies conducted. Unfortunately for me, the unlikely need for a sub investigator had materialized. I needed Dr. Jones to assess this result and decide the best course of treatment for the patient. What was also unfortunate? The abnormal results were for the elderly gentleman I had first screened for the pneumonia study. He had entrusted us with his treatment, and it may have caused further illness. I know he signed consent, and he knew the possible risks, but I still felt guilty.

I knew what I had to do. I picked up the telephone to have Dr. Jones paged. It was his day off, but I would gladly risk his frustration to ensure that the patient was provided the best medical care. I waited in Dr. Smith's office until her telephone rang. Jenna patched the call from Dr. Jones through to me. "Yes, this is Dr. Jones" he began. I swallowed and began my explanation. "Dr. Jones, I am sorry to bother you. This is Dr. Smith's research nurse. As you know she is out of town this week..." I quickly explained the study patient's elevated lab results and his age, background and relevant medical history. Dr. Jones asked about the study treatment. I explained that the pneumonia study was a double blind, comparator pneumonia study that compared our investigational antibiotic to a standard antibiotic in a one-to-one randomization scheme.

Dr. Jones instructed me to contact the patient immediately for a study visit, to optimally occur this afternoon, or the very next morning. He cautioned me to inform the patient of the importance of returning to the clinic as soon as possible, without alarming the patient unnecessarily. He provided some last minute instruction about his office scheduling process, and then surprised me with a compliment. "Lisa, you were right to call me. Nice work. I will see you when I get in." I hung up the telephone, surprised by the content and outcome of the conversation with Dr. Jones. It was our first interaction, and it gone remarkably well. He was professional, effective, and kind. I knew I had done the right thing in contacting him the minute I saw the lab result. However, his final words validated my decision and helped strengthen my sometimes shaky confidence in my judgment.

I picked up the telephone to contact the study patient. After identifying myself, I calmly explained that we needed to see him in the clinic as soon as possible due to some abnormal test results. I let him know that we would provide additional details after we completed more tests and examined him in person. "I always look forward to seeing you girls. You take such good care of me" was his simple reply. I further explained that Dr. Smith was out of town, but that her colleague, Dr. Jones, would be treating him. Though he sounded initially calm, his next question demonstrated his anxiety. "Will you be there?" he asked. I promised him that I would meet him in the lobby and be by his side throughout the entire visit. He was appreciative of this. We were thankfully able to schedule him for an early morning visit, the following day.

After the final steps in organizing the patient's return visit were completed, I returned to my office and nearly fell into my chair. I was emotionally drained by the events of the morning, but still had mounds of paperwork to complete, as a result of the patient's elevated lab result and unscheduled visit. Jenna's quick thinking, and my thorough training, had helped discover a potential health problem and plan of attack for the study patient. The reason for the elevated lab result was unknown at this point. It could be an unrelated acute condition, hemolyzed blood that affected the result, etiology of his pneumonia, or a study drug related SAE. The patient may need to be hospitalized and his drug treatment unblinded to determine appropriate medical intervention, or removed from the study. None of that mattered. With our quick action, we had preserved the safety and best interests of the study patient, which was the highest priority in the research process. I had learned well from my mentor.

# CHAPTER
# 11

## THE FIRST IMPRESSION IS NOT THE BEST IMPRESSION.

The monitor assigned to our sinusitis study (Suzanne) intimidated me; it was as simple as that. With stern, blue eyes framed by thick glasses, she resembled a cross between a TV reporter and my kindergarten teacher. My opinion was based solely on the first impression she made (unfair I know), and unfortunately influenced by Jane's attitude toward monitors. Jane was biased against all monitors, for she could not bear anyone finding fault in her work. When I first started at the clinic, Jane had warned me to be wary of them all. However, I would later learn what an asset a good monitor was to any investigational site, as their review of our records helped produce credible study data.

Jane was the supervisor of the study nurses, so they fortunately emulated her treatment of study patients, and unfortunately, her treatment of monitors. Thus the nurses provided the highest level of patient care and demonstrated a less than helpful attitude toward their monitors. Jane perceived all monitors as auditors at an FDA site inspection, with a primary goal to identify errors. This attitude trickled down to the study nurses she supervised. She would instruct the nurses to complete no more than basic work required to fulfill the monitor's commitments and study deadlines during a visit. Asking a study nurse to stay late during a monitoring visit was unheard of, and requesting an extra monitoring day at "Jane's" clinic was not well met. This behavior made the difficult job of monitoring even more challenging, and caused the monitors to sometimes feel resentful towards the research nurses. It was a counter-productive cycle that benefitted no one, though I did not understand it at the time.

The first order of business when Dr. Smith returned from her last minute trip, (her grandmother had died) was to schedule a monitoring visit for our sinusitis study. She had arranged for the monitor to come to our site the day before the official visit to review the CRFs and create the corrections needed to expedite data retrieval. Seven patients had been enrolled in the study, which was a small number and allowed the monitor to finish her data corrections in that short of a timeframe.

The official monitoring visit (with me) started on Tuesday at 9 am. Dr. Smith had really prepared for this visit. All sinusitis study patient records had been delivered to my office, and all study patient source documents were filed next to the case report forms on my desk. I felt we were ready, and I was excited to finally start work on this study. However, when Suzanne and I met, she returned my smile with a grimace, and my enthusiasm with her cold formality. I began to wonder if Jane's attitude toward monitors was warranted. Though I had technically worked with another monitor, Eric, I did not count that as a "real" monitoring experience. He was paid to train me and to be nice to me. This was my first, authentic monitoring visit. The start did not bode well for things to come.

When Dr. Smith left us to our work, I did not know whether to expect pleasant conversation or leg irons to precede the work load. Suzanne did not disappoint. Her instructions were curt, and her words of encouragement nonexistent. "We have a lot of work to do," she barked as she handed me a large pile of monitoring correction forms for the sinusitis case report books. The study had been admittedly neglected, but certainly not due to my laziness or disinterest. When I took on this large workload, I had to prioritize my tasks. This study had stopped enrolling, and the patients were in various stages of follow up, which meant enrolling studies with immediate deadlines took precedence. I had barely glanced at the patient case books before the visit. I had been hoping for some understanding, some direction, from Suzanne. I had hoped in vain. I attempted to explain this to Suzanne, but she did not appear to care. She informed me that no matter the circumstances, the work still had to be completed as soon as possible. She said that she would check on my progress after lunch and left me to my own devices.

## SO MUCH FOR KIND INSTRUCTION

I took the pile of monitoring correction forms back to my desk. They were three-layer carbon copy forms, with written instructions that corresponded to the specific CRF page and what data needed to be corrected, or changed. Once the corrections were resolved on the correction form and corresponding CRF, Suzanne would pull the top two pages of both forms and sent them into her company's data management department for review. The site kept the bottom copies of both the correction form and CRF page. The final, most important part of the data retrieval process.

I reviewed the first correction form. Suzanne's writing was neat, and her instruction, thankfully, clear. I grabbed the corresponding patient CRF and source documents, so I could complete the corrections. I studied the documents and discovered that this patient had discontinued from the study and still needed an early term visit. I had a sinking feeling that this was not the only patient with this unfinished status. I opened two more case books, and found two more study patients three months overdue for their last study visit. I sighed in frustration, and decided to perform a high level review of all case books to assess the status. Out of seven total study patients, three had outstanding final visits, three patients had completed the study, but had missing study drug, and one patient had discontinued the study without the early term visit completed. Seven patients to track down for follow up; a monumental task, but, nothing new for me. It would be challenging to successfully schedule and complete final follow up visits for these patients, in Suzanne's deadline, but I would do my best.

I then started the correction process. To my relief, the remaining edits were relatively straightforward. Such as, hypertension medication noted as a concomitant medication in the source documents, but hypertension was not noted as a corresponding medical history item. Adverse events were noted in the CRF, but needed to be confirmed in the medical record and source documents. Physical exam and diagnostic lab/ECG results required CRF entry. I spent the entire morning working on the corrections and made substantial progress. And Suzanne had contributed to the efficiency. She had written each correction to ensure the action required for resolution was clear. Her queries were logical, well-crafted and easy to understand. Perhaps she was not so bad after all.

As promised, at lunch time, Suzanne came back to check on my progress. I really wanted to impress her, to show her that I was willing to work hard and learn. Our working relationship would be so much easier if she would stop judging me for the bad habits of my predecessor and develop faith in my skills as a study nurse. Before Suzanne could start glaring, I started explaining my plan to recapture patients lost to follow up. I informed her that I had found all patient contact information in the regulatory binder, and that I was going to spend tomorrow tracking patients down, convincing them to return for their final study visit. I let her know that I had done this successfully for another study that had patients lost to follow up. I felt confident I would have the same results with her study, and in time for her deadline. After this explanation, I waited for any positive sign of acknowledgement, or response, from Suzanne. She just kept staring at me, assessing me, as if she were looking for something. I was starting to feel uncomfortable. And then out of the blue, she surprised me again. "I can come in tomorrow to help you contact the patients, if that would help." Though she was not smiling when she said this, she was not glaring. That was significant to me. I wanted to leap up and give her a big hug for her kindness, but I dare not. She might karate chop me or spray me with mace.

I had won a small victory today. Developing a positive relationship with Suzanne would be a long process. My predecessor had caused her a lot of pressure and grief with the incomplete work and study status. I would have to convince Suzanne, and the monitors, that I was committed, focused, and in for the long haul. Relationship development took time, but it was well worth the effort. I kept my response simple. "Thank you, Suzanne. That would be great!" She looked embarrassed as she returned to her work area. I felt relieved as I went back to my corrections.

# CHAPTER

## 12

## MY FIRST INVESTIGATOR'S MEETING.

At precisely 8:22 am, on the morning of my three month anniversary as a study coordinator, Dr. Smith strolled into my office, grinning like a Cheshire cat. For a brief moment, I was touched. She must have remembered that today was the end of my three-month probationary period, and was here to congratulate me… A sweet, but short lived dream. "Lisa, we are going to our first investigator's meeting!" Was that excitement I heard in her normally placid tone of voice? That great news well made up for any disappointment I may have felt over the forgotten anniversary.

Investigator's meetings signaled the official start of any study. They were large training meetings attended by all investigational site staff selected to participate in the pending study. They were usually held in grand hotels, in cosmopolitan cities, and offered a full indoctrination to the study design, objectives, and requirements. There was also the exciting opportunity to network with other study sites and investigators (some famous). A recreational excursion, be it a large dinner at an exclusive restaurant, or tickets to a local landmark/amusement park/ event, was included for the attendees, as a respite/reward from the often long and grueling training that comprised the meeting. I had overheard the other study nurses discussing the meetings, and how much fun they were. I never dreamed that I would have the opportunity to attend one so soon. I was a little confused, however. I had taken over several studies, in various stages of enrollment or follow up. None of them was brand new. This study appeared, quite literally, out of the blue.

Dr. Smith explained the circumstances of the investigator's meeting for the mysterious influenza study we were about to start. I rolled my eyes, inwardly. Enough with viruses and infections. Why couldn't we conduct a fun, and clean study, maybe for a new skin treatment or weight supplement? Now that would be right up my alley. I turned my attention back to Dr. Smith and the important details. My predecessor had completed a portion of the study start-up, regulatory documents before she left, and Jane had been charged with their completion. We had just received IRB approval for the study. Jane had worked diligently on this, which surprised me. Maybe there was hope for their relationship after all.

Dr. Smith had wisely decided not to include me in any of this paperwork, as she did not want to overwhelm me any more than necessary. The timing was perfect. The studies I had assumed were relatively under control (relatively being the key word here-open to interpretation and status change). I could handle the addition of another one, especially since two of the studies I was currently managing were close to closing, with data retrieved and all patients having completed their final study visit. I was really looking forward to starting a study from the beginning. It would be my first opportunity to participate in a trial from inception to close, and all of the pivotal points in between. I would influence patient screening, patient selection, monitoring process and conduct, with my choices, my attention, and my enthusiasm. I would not have to follow and fix someone else's mess.

The investigator's meeting was scheduled to occur from Thursday to Saturday; in about two weeks' time. It was not a lot of notice, but sufficient enough to prepare myself. It was not as if I had a life anyway!! Dr. Smith explained that her secretary would arrange the travel and advised me to book the flight to leave early Thursday morning, as the meeting was in Florida. Florida!! How exciting! I had visions of training meetings occurring poolside, with investigational staff sprawled on sun chairs and floating couches, while we listened to the sponsor medical monitor explain the latest strain of the flu virus, while sipping a fruity drink. Like that would happen. From what I had gleaned from the other study nurses, during training, all of the meeting attendees would be ensconced, coffin like, in a conference room, with the requisite freezing temperature to ensure attendees stayed awake. Meanwhile, a very dry, monotone sponsor representative droned on about protocol and investigational product data. But it was still an investigator's meeting, and it was still with Dr. Smith!! I floated through the rest of the day. I was traveling with my famous mentor to our first study meeting. We would finally have a chance to spend some uninterrupted time together, where I could soak up her knowledge, experience, and see her in action among her colleagues at the meeting. Things were finally coming together in a most wonderful way!

The next morning, I retrieved a travel itinerary and meeting agenda from Dr. Smith's secretary. We were due to arrive in Florida late Thursday afternoon, in time for the "Welcome" dinner for all meeting attendees. The dinner was at the hotel restaurant, which I had already checked out online. The hotel was rated highly, and looked beautiful. The official study meeting started Friday morning at 8am, and concluded at 5 pm. Ugh, that was going to be a long day. Our first "event" was an hour after the training ended. It was set at a mystery dinner theater, with an interactive, "who dunnit" story line. The diners were part of the play and assisted the actors in the mock murder investigation. I had never attended a mystery dinner theater; attending with Dr. Smith would be an adventure, indeed. I imagined she would be answering emails on her smart phone throughout the dinner. Wouldn't it be great if she was chosen to be a play participant? Now, I would get a kick out of that.

The training on Saturday morning was set from 9-1pm. We were scheduled to fly home at 4 pm that afternoon. Short and sweet. I secretly willed Dr. Smith to book us business class tickets, but the thrifty sponsor would only pay for attendees to fly coach. I then prepared a mental to do list and set about preparing for this big event.

The two week period passed in a blur of wonderful, euphoric stress. I managed to locate the start-up study document file, read the entire study protocol and schedule of events, and briefly review the investigator site manual. The study design was straightforward, with a short screening and treatment period. Study patients were given an intramuscular injection of either study drug, or matching placebo. All study patients were treated with the best supportive care, e.g. acetaminophen and expectorants as needed. All patients were assessed for safety and efficacy via follow up visits that included blood work, physical exams, ECGs and patient questionnaires. All patients had a final study visit, and then a follow up phone call two weeks later. Now, this I understood. This was a study I could literally sink my teeth into. I had committed the protocol to memory, and had done all possible preparation for the meeting, short of crafting a thank you letter to the pharmaceutical company for this opportunity.

On Thursday morning, (the day we were scheduled to leave) my alarm startled me out of a deep sleep. I had spent the first part of the night worrying about missing our 6:30am flight; I had finally fallen asleep at 2am. I peered at the electronic alarm display as I struggled to wake up. 3:45 am. Brilliant. Almost two hours of sleep. This was going to be a rough morning. But as I started the hot shower, and grabbed my first of twelve cups of coffee, a rush of realization and excitement hit me. I was going to Florida for my first study meeting. I was going to bond with Dr. Smith. I was going to spend the weekend at a swanky hotel. I was finally off of probation. HALLELUIAH!!

After my fifth cup of coffee, I was ready to leave for the airport. Being such an ungodly hour, traffic was nonexistent. The airport was equally quiet. I literally sailed through ticketing and security. Dr. Smith and I were scheduled to meet in the boarding area an hour before departure. It was 5am, so I decided to grab a latte and read over the protocol. I sat in the nearly empty gate area, nursing my latte and waiting anxiously for my investigator to arrive. I waited, and waited, crossed my legs, organized my notes, categorized my stickies and waited some more. Still no sign of Dr. Smith. At 5:45am, I was at full worry mode. At 6 am, just as I was reaching for my phone to make the dreaded call, it started to ring. With a sinking feeling I saw that it was Dr. Smith.

"Hello" was my hesitant greeting. "Lisa" said Dr. Smith in a solemn voice. "I have bad news." She went onto explain that her youngest daughter was ill with the flu and she could not come to the meeting. I was devastated. She then began the requisite encouragement speech. I listened in dejection. "Lisa, you will be fine without me. You have done such a great job learning everything. I have no doubt that you will have a great time at the meeting. I am so sorry I cannot come." I nodded, and she continued her explanation. She instructed me to find a sponsor representative at the hotel, who would provide me with an agenda and schedule of events for the meeting. She concluded the conversation with an apology, and asked me to call her if I needed anything. Her kind words buoyed my spirits, but I was still crestfallen. So much for attending the meeting with my famous mentor; so much for the much needed bonding time; so much for mingling and making important contacts for the practice. What could I do on my own? I was only one person, and clueless at that. I did not have the confidence to mix and mingle at such a meeting. I lacked Dr. Smith's experience, persuasion. She could persuade Genghis Khan to attend a bridal shower. I had to use free coffee and donuts to bribe senior citizens to drive two blocks for a final study visit.

I slumped in my seat, and was embarrassed to feel tears clouding my vision. I was still in shock over what had just taken place. I was traveling across the country, alone, to the extremely important (and my first) investigator's meeting. All of my excitement and anticipation vanished, replaced with angst and frustration. Why couldn't anything go smoothly with this job? In the midst of my dejection, I felt someone staring at me. It was a woman seated in a chair directly behind, and to the left, of where I was sitting. I looked around at her, and she smiled sympathetically at me. That struck me as a little odd, and a lot creepy. I did not need another complicated situation to deal with, such as a crazy stranger in an airport. The woman then rose, and walked slowly towards me. I did not quite know how to react. She asked if she could sit down, and I nodded uncomfortably. The next words out of her mouth shocked me out of my sadness. "I couldn't help but overhear that conversation. You must be going to the investigator's meeting in Orlando. So am I." These words made me feel a little more hopeful. Perhaps she wasn't crazy after all.

# CHAPTER

## 13

## A FRIEND IN DISGUISE.

The words poured out of my mouth before my filter could kick in. I found myself explaining everything to this woman. "My boss just called to tell me that her daughter has the flu, and she can't make it to the meeting." She nodded in understanding. "I have only been a study nurse for three months. I just learned how to do my job, and still have more to learn. How am I supposed to attend this meeting alone?" Why was I pouring my heart out to this complete stranger? Because she had ears, was willing to listen, and I desperately needed someone to talk to. Were she not around, I would have resorted to confiding in the housekeeper emptying the trashcans.

She shook her head in understanding. "I am so sorry. I know how devastating this is. I have been through the same thing myself." I could not believe my ears, that someone sitting across the boarding area from me had experienced the same situation. She introduced herself as Tommi. She was a study coordinator from a dedicated research site in North County, on her way to attend the same investigator's meeting in Orlando. Her principal investigator was notably absent. "I was not trying to eavesdrop," she explained, "but when I overheard you talking to your boss, I just had to say something. I knew exactly how you felt." I felt thankful for her eavesdropping, intentional or not. I really needed her guidance.

Her reassurance was as straightforward as her personality. "Dr. Smith couldn't help this happening. I know she feels bad leaving you alone. But she knows that you can take care of yourself." I looked up at her. "She has done so much for me. I just wanted to show her how much I have learned." I said this with all sincerity. "And I am sure you have done just as much for her." Tommi's words gave me pause and made me think. I had worked really hard for Dr. Smith. I had come so far in such a short amount of time. I knew I had so much more to learn, but perhaps attending this meeting alone would cause me to rely more on myself, and less on my wonderful employer. Tommi provided additional clarity and reassurance. "You really don't need a babysitter at these meetings. There is so much to learn, and so much going on, that there isn't any time to worry." She smiled kindly at me. "Plus, I would be happy to show you around. My doctor is not coming either."

I smiled, for I was starting to feel better about things. This Tommi person, whom I first suspected was crazy, may turn out to be my rational saving grace. She was direct, funny, and more importantly, experienced. I felt less nervous, and very grateful, to have an unexpected ally in my camp.

We continued talking until they boarded the plane. We managed to switch our seat assignments, and sat next to each other on the flight to Orlando. We spent the entire flight discussing our love for clinical research and how we came to work in this field. Tommi's history was fascinating to me. She had been a study coordinator for eight years, and worked for a successful research organization with many sites around the West. The principal investigator she worked for had been unable to attend several investigator meetings due to scheduling conflicts (such as golf, surfing, golf, surfing and golf, not necessarily in that order). This gave Tommi the preferred option of exploring cities than having to entertain her quirky boss, aka the "brilliant surfer" as she good naturedly referred to him.

Tommi described a working situation that was pleasant but isolated. Her supervising physician was a internal medicine doctor who had graduated with top honors from Stanford, was an incredibly conscientious and involved investigator, was a dream to work with (no micromanagement, he was more inclined to trust people to their own autonomy until he was proven wrong) but was a bit of an eccentric outdoorsman who took every available opportunity to golf, surf or hike. He drove a VW bus and wore tropical print shirts to work; they literally had to force him into a suit and out of his flip flops for these meetings. Her working relationship with her colleagues was another story. Tommi had worked at the research center for less than a year, with a group of women who had collectively worked at the clinic for greater than twenty five years. They were a tight-knit group, and Tommi never felt as though she fit in with them. She spoke bluntly and carried herself with a confidence that surely intimidated these women. I, however, always found directness refreshing, after dealing with some passive-aggressive personalities at the clinic. Tommi and I instantly clicked. Our conversation was easy and flowed, making the five-hour flight to Orlando pass rapidly.

Tommi explained that the meetings were comprised of an interesting array of investigational and sponsor staff. Brilliant and bored academic investigators, doctors hungry for trials and contacts, and small town primary care physicians who were so friendly that you wanted to pack them away in your suitcase and take them home with you after the meeting. Then there were the study coordinators/nurses. I laughed out loud at her description of the study coordinators. They ranged from extremely experienced site managers with a group of study coordinators in tow (they traveled in packs) to the research naïve study coordinators completely out of their element and frightened to death (me) to the fairly experienced, fairly bored study coordinators who wanted to work a little and play A LOT at these meetings. It sounded so interesting and exciting.

66

We continued chatting until the plane landed, and proceeded to the baggage terminal to catch the hotel shuttle. At 4:30 in the afternoon, it was still ninety degrees outside, with the air as thick as mud from the Florida humidity. The shuttle bus was crowded, and I felt fatigue kick in from the long travel and emotional upheaval of the morning. I longed to lie down on a comfortable bed in a freezing-cold room. However, when we arrived at the hotel, I was invigorated by the scene before me. The hotel foyer was all glass and marble, complete with vaulted ceilings, ornate chandeliers, and bored, slightly haughty hotel staff. A group of very professional looking people milled in the front lobby area. The sponsor meeting check-in table, with the familiar study logo, was expertly placed to the left of the main check-in counter. Two pharmaceutical sales representatives were distributing meeting folders and checking in the attendees. As I surveyed the room, I began to really "see" the characters so expertly described by Tommi.

There was the small town primary care physician, and a young, eager sub-investigator, speaking enthusiastically on the settee in the middle of the lobby.

Then came the study coordinators. There was the stern site manager, with thick glasses, severe frown, accompanied by an obviously terrified nurse trainee.

Two middle-aged women were walking stealthily towards the hotel elevator, hoping to remain unnoticed as they bypassed the boring meet and greet, to catch up on some needed sleep before the evening's festivities.

Finally, I spotted the academic physician, a well dressed, slightly bored looking, older gentleman, leaning against the wall as if he had seen it all and would rather be anywhere but here.

I could not believe three months had already passed. I was the stereotypical, brand new study nurse, nervous, overwhelmed, but SO EXCITED to finally be here.

Tommi smiled fondly at my expression, for she had been there herself a while back. She placed a reassuring hand on my shoulder. "Come on, let's go check in."

I smiled and took my first pivotal step into this new world of science, of medical innovation and incredible opportunity...to meet famous medical researchers, to learn from brilliant scientists. Though they were a million steps ahead of me, we all had one small, but important, thing in common. We were all in pursuit of that miracle cure for the patients we treated. I could not wait for the next exciting step.